A Nose

Written by Sharon Wohl
Illustrated by Lisa Bradley

Printed in the U.S.A.

A Better Way of Learning • *www.phonicsgame.com*

A nose
can bump.

A nose can slant.

This nose
can smell,

but this
nose can't.

This man will tan.
His nose will not.

His nose will chill.
His feet feel hot.

This nose can sneeze.
This nose can drip.
This nose is red.
This nose is sick.

A nose can trick.
A nose can treat.
A nose can smell
a treat that's sweet.

This nose is big.
This nose is wide.
This nose can be
a fun, fast slide.